The Unpredictable Wind

THE UNPREDICTABLE WIND

A Book on the Holy Spirit

C. Brandon Rimmer and
Bill Brown

Thomas Nelson, Inc., Publishers
New York / Nashville / Camden

Copyright © 1972 by C. Brandon Rimmer and Bill Brown
All rights reserved under International and Pan-American Conventions.
Published by Thomas Nelson, Inc., Nashville, Tennessee.
Manufactured in the United States of America
All Scripture quotations, unless otherwise noted, are from the Revised Standard Version of the Bible.
This book was originally published in 1972 by Aragorn Books, Inc., Glendale, California.

Library of Congress Cataloging in Publication Data

Rimmer, Charles Brandon, 1917–
   The unpredictable wind.

   1. Holy Spirit.   I. Brown, Bill 1928–   joint author.
II. Title.
BT121.2.R56   1974   231'.3   74–23589
ISBN 0–8407–5578–3

Dedicated to some new wineskins in Detroit.

Table of Contents

xi	Introduction
1	What Is a Who?
13	He, Who Was Promised, Comes
23	Life Because of the Spirit
39	The Spirit in Us
49	Life in the Spirit
63	Gifts from the Spirit
81	The Spirit in the Fellowship
95	The Spirit and the Law

The wind blows wherever it wants to and you cannot tell from where it came, nor do you know where it is going. So is he who is carried along by the Spirit.

Jesus

Introduction

This book is written for those who are trying to follow Jesus. It is about the Holy Spirit. (Old-fashioned Bibles call Him the "Holy Ghost," a fifteenth-century word.) He is important to you in the life you share because of Jesus. Directly or indirectly, all we know about Jesus comes through Him. His primary function in this world, and maybe in the next, is to make Jesus and the nature of Jesus real to us. We hope and pray that the book will be a blessing to you.

There are a couple of things this book is not. It is not a polemic; that is, we don't mean it to be used as a club with which you bat your brother over the head if he disagrees with you. We have not assembled "proof texts" with that in mind.

Also, this is not a systematic theology. We do not for a moment propose that when you have read this, you will know all that Scripture teaches about the Holy Spirit. What we hope is that you will know something about Him—who He is and how He works in your life to enable you to follow Jesus.

We are going to assume the Trinitarian view of the Godhead. Down through the ages and at the present time there are some wonderful Christians who do not begin with this assumption, but most of those who have followed Jesus in the last two thousand years have talked about "God the Father, God the Son, and God the Holy Spirit, equal in power and glory." If you want "a head trip" that defends this assumption, we recommend *Beyond Personality* by C. S. Lewis. It is now included in *Mere Christianity*. We are going to start our first chapter with something he says.

1. What Is a Who?

What is the Holy Spirit? Is it simply a spirit or an attitude of holiness? C. S. Lewis suggests that a social club may have a spirit or personality all its own, which spirit is more than and different from the sum total of the personalities of those who make up its membership. He thinks that the Holy Spirit may be that different personality which results from the union, the fellowship, the intimate association of God the Father and God the Son. This can be helpful if you really understand it.

Can you remember enough of your high school geometry to know that if you draw two isosceles right triangles with a common hypotenuse you make a square? You draw only two figures, two triangles, but something else comes into existence. Although the square is the product of the triangles (no additional lines need be drawn), the square has characteristics different from the triangles and an existence of its own. In C. S. Lewis's illustration this point must be seen. The "spirit" of the club is an ontological entity, or in common English it is a real and separate thing brought into existence by the social club. The relationship between the Father and the Son brings into existence the Holy Spirit, separate and a person. If this is helpful, fine; if not, forget it and go on. More important to us is how His nature affects us and how He uses us.

We believe that the Spirit is a person because the Scripture gives Him the characteristics of a person. In Ephesians 4:30, He can be grieved. In Genesis 6:3, He strives. In Matthew 3:16, He takes on a bodily form. In Matthew 4:1, He leads. In John 3:5, He gives birth. In Acts 10:19, He speaks. In Romans 8:16, He bears witness. In 1 Corinthians 12, He gives gifts, and so forth. These and many more are characteristics of a person or a personality. If a man talks about something and says it broods, gives gifts, thinks, leads, changes, speaks, and so forth, he is going to lead us into thinking that he is talking about a person. This is what the Scripture does for us.

Scripture not only treats Him as a person, but as God also. Hebrews 9:14 tells us that He is eternal,

What Is a Who?

and who is eternal but God? Peter 3:18 tells us that it was He who raised Jesus from the dead, and who can give life but God? Psalm 139:7-10 tells us that He is everywhere, and who is omnipresent but God? First Corinthians 2:10-11 tells us that He knows all things, even the deep things of God, and to whom are all these things known except to God Himself? An even better indication of the deity of the Holy Spirit might be in the instruction given to the disciples concerning baptism. In Matthew 28:19 Jesus Himself says to baptize in the name of the Father, the Son, and the Holy Spirit. In His ministry, Jesus upheld the deity of the Father and identified Himself with this deity. It is difficut to see why He would include the Holy Spirit in the same way and in the same function without presupposing the same nature for the Holy Spirit. This then is the basis for the rest of our thinking. He is a person; He is God, a position which has been called "orthodox" down through history.

The best background for the study of the Holy Spirit is found in the words of Jesus to His disciples shortly before He went to the cross. He was encouraging them to help them face His coming departure. These words are in the Gospel of John, chapters thirteen through seventeen. Let us look at three passages in particular.

In John 14:16-17 Jesus says: "I will pray to the Father, and he will give you another Counselor, to be with you for ever, even the Spirit of truth, whom the world cannot receive, because it neither sees him nor knows him; you know him, for he dwells with you, and will be in you."

John 14:26: "The Counselor, the Holy Spirit, whom the Father will send in my name, he will teach you all things, and bring to your remembrance all that I have said to you."

John 16:7-15: "It is to your advantage that I go away, for if I do not go away, the Counselor will not come to you; but if I go, I will send him to you. And when he comes, he will convince [confute*] the world of sin and of righteousness and judgment: of sin, because they do not believe in me; of righteousness, because I go to the Father, and you will see me no more; of judgment, because the ruler of this world is judged.

"I have yet many things to say to you, but you cannot bear them now. When the Spirit of truth comes, he will guide you into all the truth; for he will not speak on his own authority, but whatever he hears he will speak, and he will declare to you the things that are to come. He will glorify me, for he will take what is mine and declare it to you. All that the Father has is mine; therefore I said that he will take what is mine and declare it to you."

From the verses above, we can see that the work of the Spirit is twofold. He has the ministry of comfort or advocacy, of counseling, and of teaching the believer. At the same time, He has a ministry of testimony and reproof toward the unbelieving world. Every man in the world is under one of these two functions of the Holy Spirit (John 1:9).†

Let us look at the negative functions. First, "Of sin, because they do not believe in me." If the whole world were dying of cancer and a doctor invented a drug that would cure it, those who refused to take the medicine would be in some measure responsible for their sickness. The world is full of hate and death and suicidal warfare. The rules for ending all these are set forth in the Sermon on the Mount in Matthew, chapters 5, 6, and 7. Not only the rules but the power to put them into effect is promised right along with them. The men of the first-century world, in a representative sense acting on behalf of us all, put to death the "Man who invented the medicine." The prescription still stands. It is still ignored. This "ignoring" is sin. It is sin in an individual sense when an individual "ignores." It is sin in a collective sense in that all mankind together "ignores" and is therefore apart from its Creator, separated from God.

Second, "Of righteousness, because I go to the Father, and you will see me no more." In other words, Jesus did not die in the sense of staying dead. He went with the Father and is able to show it. Down through the ages, men have found that Jesus rose from the dead, that He is alive. If this is true, He had to be righteous. Those who sin, according to the Scripture and human experience, stay dead.

Third, "Of judgment, because the ruler of this world is judged (proven wrong)." Satan had an argument, and he had standing before God because of it. It is described in the first chapter of the Book of Job: "No man, granted freedom of choice, will always choose the will of his Creator over his own best temporal interests" (authors' paraphrase). In the end even Job sinned, and Satan's argument stood. But no more does it do so. One man, Jesus, in spite of a humiliating life and an agonizing death, never once chose His own way or His own interests over the Father's. When Satan now says, "No man can do it," God can say, "One man did," and Satan is proven wrong.

Now let's look at the affirmative ministry: to comfort, to counsel (or be an advocate for), and to teach the believer. Many a man can give intellectual assent to the story of Jesus and, in one sense of the word, believe. He can believe about Him and still be apart from God. It is the work of the Holy Spirit to bring us into the relationship with Jesus that spells Life (1 Cor. 12:3):

"No one can say 'Jesus is Lord' except by the Holy Spirit." We cannot let go of the controls over ourselves and our lives and submit to Jesus as we should

What Is a Who?

unless the Holy Spirit gives us the power. We cannot continue to submit without His help. ". . . but by my spirit saith the Lord. . ." We cannot even pray without His acting as our Advocate or attorney before the throne of God (Rom 8:26).

The Holy Spirit and two things which He uses form the basis of the "Christian" walk. "This is he who came by water and blood, Jesus Christ, not with the water only but with the water and the blood. And the Spirit is the witness, because the Spirit is the truth. There are three witnesses, the Spirit, the water, and the blood" (1 John 5:6ff.).

May we be permitted an analogy? A three-legged stool has a steadiness about it. (Once again, if you remember your high school geometry, "Three points determine a plane.") A healthy follower of Jesus should be using all three legs: the Spirit, water, and the blood.

Notice that he says, "Not with the water only." John the Baptizer, who preceded Jesus, came with water only. He told Israel to get ready for the Messiah, the Coming One, and to do it by being baptized for the remission of sins. Baptism is an old Jewish custom to which Jesus gave new significance. A Jew or proselyte was immersed in the river to show God that he wanted a new start in life. It was a way of admitting publicly that one was a sinner. The New Testament has enriched it. Paul teaches that we are baptized into the death of Jesus. The new life, therefore, is not an attempt to live a more "moral" life, but to live out the new kind of life—the Life of Jesus that the Spirit puts within us.

There is one more use of the word "water" that we must consider. Jesus uses it in reference to His words. They also wash. "You are already made clean by the word which I have spoken to you" (John 15:3). In Scripture, "water and the word" are not strangers to each other. To immerse one's heart and mind, with the help of the Spirit, in the words of Jesus is a way to get a mental and spiritual bath. We should not try to follow Jesus without seeing what He's like through the words that He spoke.

Water baptism, as a symbol of repentance, and the study of the Scripture are together a tool of the Holy Spirit, and when used by Him they are life giving and sometimes indispensable. But they are only one leg of His stool, and a one-legged stool is a difficult thing upon which to try to take one's stand.

There is also the blood, "not with the water only but with the water and the blood." From Genesis to Revelation two things, among others, are preached. The wages of sin are death, and without the shedding of blood there is no forgiveness of sin. The moral law was broken, and the penalty was paid by the blood of Christ. This is a foundation stone of our faith, but not the subject at hand. We are looking at

What Is a Who?

the blood in terms of the ministry of the Holy Spirit. We find it in 1 John 1:7, ". . . but if we walk in the light as He is in the light, we share a common life, and the flood of His son Jesus is cleansing us from all sin . . ." (authors' paraphrase) (note the present progressive tense, "is cleansing").

Remember the Last Supper? In chapter 13 of John's Gospel, Jesus and the disciples went to the baths, bathed, and walked to the building where they were to have their final supper. It was not possible to walk twenty paces on those dirty streets without making your sandaled feet filthy and uncomfortable. When the disciples got to the room and took their places around the table, Jesus rose from His place and did for all of them what they should have done for Him and for each other. He washed their feet. When Jesus got to Peter's feet, Peter's self-righteousness, posing as modesty, came shining through. "Not my feet, Lord, you'll never wash my feet."

Jesus answered, "If you don't let me wash your feet you are 'out of the scene'."

It is no different today. As we walk the streets of our world with our hand in the hand of Jesus, we get our moral feet morally dirty, or to put it more bluntly, we sin. If we say we don't sin, we make God a liar (1 John 1:10). The Holy Spirit takes the blood of Jesus and cleans our "feet" of all dirt, even that which we do not know is there, because we cannot see it.

In some measure, we are responsible for the cleansing of the sin we can see. "If we confess our sins [the ones we can see], he is faithful and just and will forgive our sins *and* cleanse us from all unrighteousness [the ones we can't see] . . ." (1 John 1:9, authors' italics). This is if our hand is in His and we are walking in obedience to Him.

There is the third leg of this three-legged stool, and that leg is the Spirit Himself. The remainder of this book is about Him and His relationship to us.

---

*"Confute" is the better word. It means to refute successfully, to prove something to be false or invalid.

†It is the belief of many Christians that even in far-off lands and cultures, the Spirit of God deals with men in terms of their own context. The individual's response to this dealing can lead to the ultimate use of the name of Christ or to spiritual death (Rom. 2:14-16).

2. He, Who Was Promised, Comes

The gifts and the blessings of God can be different from God Himself, but it is not always so. When He wants to really bless, He gives of Himself. As He said to Abraham, "I shall be your exceeding great reward."* When He wants to give us the blessings that are in Christ, He gives us Christ. "And this is the testimony, that God gave us eternal life, and this life is in his Son" (1 John 5:11).

With the Holy Spirit, the same pattern holds true. While there are examples of gifts being given and exercised by those who have no fellowship with the Spirit (Saul, king of Israel, for instance), such examples are exceptions. When God wants us to have the gifts or the ministries of the Holy Spirit, He gives us the Holy Spirit.

The Unpredictable Wind

As we have read in the Gospel of John, the Holy Spirit was promised. In the Book of Acts, He comes. The interesting thing is that He comes without any apparent uniformity of experience. It has been said that the only pattern in the Book of Acts concerning the giving of the Spirit is that there is no pattern.

On the surface, at least, it would seem so. In the second chapter of Acts, as the disciples were all together on the day of Pentecost, they were suddenly filled with the Holy Spirit and began to speak in other languages which were understood by Jews from all over the world who were then gathered at Jerusalem.†

This was the fulfillment of the promised coming of the Holy Spirit for which the disciples had been instructed to wait, and they understood it as such. This, then, is an example of the Holy Spirit being given after a period of waiting, fasting, and prayer.

Philip, sometimes called "the Evangelist," went to the first country north of Jerusalem (Samaria) and preached Jesus (Acts 8:5ff.). "Many believed and were baptized but they did not receive the gift of the Holy Spirit until Peter and John came up from Jerusalem and prayed for them and laid hands on them" (authors' paraphrase). There is no indication that, as in our first example, there was a period of waiting, fasting, and prayer on the part of the Samaritans. This time the gift was given through the hands of the apostles.

He, Who Was Promised, Comes

In the tenth chapter of Acts, Peter preached Jesus to some Gentiles in the house of the Roman, Cornelius. While Peter was still speaking, the Holy Spirit fell upon those who were listening—no waiting, no fasting, no period of prayer, and no laying on of hands.

Toward the end of the Book of Acts (19:1-7), Paul entered the city of Ephesus and found some disciples of John the Baptizer. The order of events in the giving of the Spirit is once again different. They were already "converts." They were preached to, baptized with water, Paul's hands were laid on them, and they received the Spirit. There is no indication in the text that they asked for Him; they had admitted that they had not even heard of Him.

At this point, we have the giving of the Spirit with and without preaching, with and without the laying on of the apostle's hand, with and without water baptism, with and without "tarrying," and so forth. In the light of all this, there should be little wonder that there is considerable disagreement about how the Spirit is given.

Combining all the elements in the Acts accounts will not help solve the problem either. We might repent, believe in the Lordship of Christ, be baptized with water, go to Jerusalem and wait around for the next Pentecost (literally, a Jewish festival occurring fifty days after the Passover), but where would we find one of the twelve to lay his hands on us? They have all been dead for almost two thousand years. This combination would be a human invention anyway, for there is no example in Scripture in which the whole program is followed.

Anyone who wishes to drop the matter of methodology at this point and say that God gives the Holy Spirit when and how He chooses has our blessing. We think we see some reasons for what went on.

We hope we are not presenting them in a spirit of dogmatism. They are put forward for your consideration, but we will not walk across the street to fight for them. They are not the foundation of fellowship.

We believe that we can understand these examples better when we see that each of these may be a first instance of the gospel being preached to and received by differing groups of people in differing circumstances. Acts 2 records the first hearing by Jews; Acts 8, the first hearing by Samaritans; Acts 10, the first hearing by Gentiles; and Acts 19, the first recorded hearing by disciples of John the Baptizer. Granted that some of these people had heard Jesus and heard about Him, but these were the first times that the gospel had been preached to these groups after the prophecies had been fulfilled.

Let's look at the groups. To the Jews at Pentecost, Peter said, "Repent, and be baptized . . . in the name of Jesus Christ for the forgiveness of sins; and you will receive the gift of the Holy Spirit" (Acts 2:38). Notice Peter does not say, "Do these things so that you may receive the Spirit," but rather, "Do these things, and you will receive the Spirit." The Jews had not asked for the Spirit but asked Peter how they might get out from under their terrible crime, the murder of Jesus. Peter stated that along with the forgiveness and cleansing they sought, they would receive the Holy Spirit for which they had not yet asked.

The Samaritans in Acts 8 believed Philip's preaching about Jesus, were baptized, and started to follow Jesus; but the Holy Spirit had fallen on none of them. The Spirit did not do so until Peter and John came down from Jerusalem and prayed for them. However, to deduce from this that men receive the Holy Spirit only when an apostle lays on his hands is to make a deduction that does not follow of necessity. It is a deduction that is contrary to other examples. We will have more to say about this Samaritan record later, but for the moment let us set it aside.

The Gentiles who received the Spirit so quickly in Acts 10 were unusual Gentiles. Notice that when Paul addresses a synagogue he talks to "Men of Israel, and you that fear God" (Acts 13:16). These "God fearers" were Gentiles who had turned their backs on the pagan religions of their own culture, and who, out of a real hunger for the true God, went to the synagogue to listen to Moses being read. This was a humiliating position for a Roman in particular and for Gentiles in general. Their pride was gone, and like the Syro-Phoenician woman (Mark 7) they would settle for crumbs from the table God had set before His own people. They were admitting in a public way that they were spiritually hungry or they would not have been there. The Spirit was poured out on them without delay.

In Acts 19, the order of events in receiving the Spirit might look like a formula, particularly if one assumes that the people involved were "believers" when Paul got to Ephesus. Look a little more closely. Here is a group which had been introduced to Paul as disciples (converts), but Paul noticed immediately that something was missing. He asked them, "Did you receive the Holy Spirit when you became believers?" When they replied that they did not even know about the Holy Spirit, he asked about their baptism and found that they were not followers of Jesus, but followers of John the Baptizer. They knew only John's baptism, which was an expression of repentance. In this they had believed, they had received that much of God's message, and within their limited understanding they were obeying, but they did not know Jesus. This was indicated to Paul by the fact that they did not even know about the Holy Spirit, not even about His existence.

Paul immediately began to explain to them that the one whose coming John the Baptizer had proclaimed and upon whom John had told them to place their trust was Jesus. They were ready, and they believed.

They put their trust in Jesus and were baptized in His name. Paul put his hands on them, and they received the Spirit.

If the problem had been a matter of the right form of baptism, Paul could have started there. If it had been a matter of the laying on of hands, Paul could have started there. If it had been a matter of tarrying and praying, Paul could have told them to do that. The problem was that they did not have the right relationship with Jesus. This is what Paul changed in order that they might receive the Spirit. The fact that there is an order to events following this is to us comparatively unimportant. We believe that any other sequence mentioned in the text would have done just as well.

What, then, can we find in these examples that can apply to our own receiving of the Holy Spirit? Perhaps one thing at least. In none of these examples does it seem apparent to us that the Holy Spirit manifested Himself to these people because they were sitting or kneeling around a room, pleading with Him to please show up.

Possibly the example of the baptism of the Jews in Jerusalem and the baptism of the disciples of John at Ephesus might be used to argue that "tarrying" is a necessary step, at least some of the time. Maybe, but look at what these things are. Repentance is not to be confused with afflicting one's self or doing some kind of penance. It is a state of mind, a changed state of mind. It comes when we realize that our attitudes, actions, and lives are wrong in God's eyes, or wrong by any other objective standard. This realization can cause us to request water baptism—not in order to "be saved" but to show that submission to God's just judgment against us has already taken place. Repentance and water baptism are simply natural responses that show publicly our regret for the ungodly quality of our lives apart from Jesus.

So far as we can see, in these instances mentioned above, those who received the Holy Spirit did so not by earnest pleading, not by following any set formula, and not by attaining an imaginary level of sinlessness in their lives. Rather, the Holy Spirit was given to those who saw themselves as lost and apart from God and therefore accepted Christ's sacrifice on their behalf and submitted themselves to the Lordship of Jesus.

---

*For those who would.

†As a matter of historical interest, there was a natural reason for the perplexity of the crowd. There was a *lingua franca*, a common language of business throughout the Roman Empire in that day. It is called *Koine Dialektos*; freely translated, the language of coinage, money, or business. It had been spread throughout the ancient world by Alexander the Great. Almost every Jew understood that language, and there was no need for every man to hear in his own local "tongue" when there was one univesal language available.

3. Life Because of the Spirit

May we call your attention to the different verbs which are used in connection with the receiving of the Holy Spirit. In the King James Version of the Bible, we find "baptized" used by Jesus on Mount Olivet. We find "filled" at Pentecost. In the Samaritan story the verb is "fallen on" until the arrival of Peter and John, and then we see the word "received." In Ephesus, the King James says that the Holy Spirit "came on" the former disciples of John the Baptizer.

We are not trying to defend the King James Version nor deprecate it, but merely point out that the English differences frequently are caused by differences in what we believe to be the original Greek text. We are not sure that these different terms should be used interchangeably. We will look at them one at a time.

First, let's look at the word "baptize." (We'll talk about "filled" in the next chapter.) In connection with the Holy Spirit, "baptized" appears first in Matthew 3:11 when John the Baptizer says: "I baptize you with water for repentance, but he who is coming after me is mightier than I; . . . he will baptize you with the Holy Spirit and with fire." In Acts 1:4-5 Jesus uses the same word in reference to the coming event at Pentecost.

The definition of "baptize" has been altered by culture. It has also been altered for some of us by a "liturgical" background. The original meaning was not "sprinkle." In classical Greek a ship was said to be "baptized" when it was sunk. Granted, in New Testament times the meaning had changed considerably, and the term seems to have meant some purposeful immersion. For instance, cloth which had been immersed in a dye vat and changed color had been "baptized" not because of the change in color necessarily, but because it had been immersed in the solution.

It is hard to think of a better description of the work of the Holy Spirit in a man who submits himself to the Lordship of Jesus. In this connection, it is interesting to note that many phrases in our

English Bible translated "believed in the Lord Jesus Christ" could be more literally translated "believed into the Lord Jesus Christ" (i.e., John 3:16). There could be a conceivable connection between the use of the preposition "into" (*eis*) Christ and the baptizing of the believer by the Holy Spirit into the body of Christ. (Romans 6 will be discussed in more detail later.)

The "natural" (pre-regenerate) man is said to be dead in sin (Eph. 2:1). He is incapable of understanding spiritual things (1 Cor. 2:14). He is also incapable of even seeing the kingdom of God (John 3:3) or of judging things concerning it.

After a man is changed by the Holy Spirit through submission to Christ (regenerated), he is a new creation (2 Cor. 5:17) and a child of God (Rom. 8:15). He looks forward to the finished work of the Spirit when he will be conformed to the image of the Lord Jesus (Rom. 8:29). It would seem reasonable to us to assume that the baptism of, with, or in (for the moment, take your choice) the Holy Spirit refers not only to His coming at Pentecost, but also to all that He accomplishes in the believer.

Now we are getting close to some "toe treading" and we would like to interject something that we hope will be helpful. There are some touchy semantic problems.

It has been our experience in dealing with new

converts that they are not always choosy about their theological vocabulary. A man who has had his first encounter with Christ may talk about being "born again," "reconciled," "regenerated," or "saved." All these words have different shades of meaning. They are not always interchangeable; however, we should pick an appropriate time and place to explain this.

If a Christian says, "I got saved last Friday night," and says it with a big smile on his face, we should not answer, "Now 'saved' is a translation of the Greek verb. . . ." The new Christian is talking about something that happened to him. He has a new relationship with God and the world around him. Leave the theological semantics out of it for a while. It is true that the subtle differences between certain words can give added insight into what God has done for us through our Lord Jesus Christ, but there is a time and a place to go into such things. It is not always twenty minutes after a man has been converted. Jesus said to give a cup of cool water, not throw it in someone's face.

What is true about conversion and the Lord can be true about the believer and the Holy Spirit. Men have had experiences with the Holy Spirit that have really "turned them on." They are filled with love and joy and are a pleasure to be near. It is not always the "right" time to start talking about theological

Life Because of the Spirit

vocabulary. Resentment is engendered in such Christians when they get the feeling that we are questioning their experience or the genuineness of their experience, because we are not accepting their "theological" description of their experience.

Some words and phrases are "loaded." There are times when "a rose by any other name" would smell the same. There are times when it is not true. For instance, if someone says, "There goes a skunk," we may hold our noses while a little pussy cat walks by. We will not risk a sniff.

Something like this has happened to the phrase, "baptism of the Holy Spirit." We believe that it has been used to cover a number of things, some very good and some not so good. To the best of our limited ability, we are going to try to stay within the New Testament use of this phrase and related phrases. The fact that we disagree with the use that other people may make of the same terms does not imply that we think they have not had contact with the Holy Spirit, nor are we implying that their experience is spurious.

Many people teach that what they call "the baptism of the Holy Spirit" takes place in a person weeks, months, or even years after the individual has accepted Jesus as his or her personal savior. These persons sometimes refer to their experience as a "second work of grace" (i.e., something the Spirit does after salvation).

We would like to say the following with great care and offend as few people as possible. Please notice that the two phrases (1) "to accept Christ as your personal savior" and (2) "a second work of grace" are two phrases that, to our knowledge, do not appear anywhere in the Bible. Paul says that his words are chosen for him by the Holy Spirit, and we think that when we ignore his meaning and make up our own phrases, we may have made up our own theology as well. Not too healthy a procedure!

In the New Testament, Jesus is the savior of the whole world (1 John 2:2). He is the Lord of those who belong to Him and follow Him (Rom. 8:14;1 John 2:3-4). Let's try a mundane illustration.

If a wealthy man walks into a jail and posts bail for all the prisoners and then says, "Come on out of jail and follow me, do as I say, and you will never come to trial," we have an analogous situation. Bail is posted for everyone, but the prisoner who likes it in jail and wants to stay there is going to face trial and condemnation whether bail was posted or not. The man who walks out and follows his benefactor has bail forfeited in lieu of his appearance. He has passed from "death into life,"

Jesus says, "I paid the price for all sin, now come on out of 'the world' (the world system) and follow me and you will never come into judgment." The man who says, "That's great. I believe," and continues to live as he lived before he heard the message is a liar (1 John 2:4). The man who says, "I believe," and then like Saul of Tarsus adds, "I was not disobedient to the heavenly vision," is on salvation's highway.

This concept of submission is not always taught as part of the basis of our relationship to Christ. It is possible, then, that some people believed in "a second work of grace" (in which they are submersed into Christ), because when they first heard that "bail was posted" they continued to sit in jail, and what they call their "second work of grace" is really their first. If it transforms their life and the image of Jesus begins to take shape in their lives (1 John 2:6), they have been dipped into God's "vat," they have been immersed into Jesus, they have been baptized by the Holy Spirit; therefore they walk in newness of life.

Notice two things. We have not said that this is the one and only experience in the life of the follower of Jesus, and we have not said that this experience is exactly the same nor "timed" the same for everyone. What we have said is that a person is baptized by the Holy Spirit when certain things transpire. Go back to the illustration of the vat and the dye. When we dye a fabric, we immerse it in the dye, and it is changed so that it is in accord with the dye. The fabric does not take on all the characteristics of the dye. It does not become a liquid, but its color becomes that of the dye. So also someone who truly believes is baptized by the Holy Spirit into Christ and receives spiritual life and moral qualities which are in accord with those of Jesus.

We believe that this is what Paul is talking about in the sixth chapter of Romans: "Do you not know that all of us who have been baptized into Christ Jesus were baptized into his death? We were buried therefore with him by baptism into death, so that as Christ was raised from the dead . . . we too might walk in newness of life."

Down through the ages, many theologians have applied this passage to water baptism. They teach what is called "baptismal regeneration." By this they mean that when a man is immersed in the water in the name of the Father, the Son, and the Holy Spirit, he is then and there identified by water baptism with the death of Christ. His new life in Christ begins as he comes out of the water. Most such theologians teach that without baptism, specifically water baptism, a man cannot belong to Christ.

We feel that this is not what the Scripture teaches. We believe that water baptism is the physical picture of a spiritual experience that has already taken place. We can think of no other explanation for Paul's attitude in the first chapter of 1 Corinthians. In it Paul boasts about the small number of people in Corinth he baptized with water. He thanks God that he did not baptize any of them except "Crispus and Gaius." If he baptized others, it seems to be so unimportant that he cannot be sure about the matter. If salvation or regeneration or uniting with Christ's death comes from water baptism, Paul's attitude toward it is inexplicable to us. Both here and in Galatians 3:27 ("Baptized into Christ, you have put him on like garments," authors' paraphrase) there is more involved than being dunked in a river. We believe Paul is talking about being baptized into Christ.*

The words that Paul uses in 1 Corinthians 1 as he talks about water baptism seem a little harsh and sarcastic. He gets that way when there is teaching separated from reality. Water baptism is a sign of a spiritual occurrence, and as such it is respected. It is commanded by the Lord. However, when men take the rite and give effectiveness to the physical act that really belongs to the Spirit, Paul is apt to have some unkind things to say.

Assuming spiritual baptizing in Romans 6 and Galatians 3, who does the baptizing? 1. Reverend "So-and-so"? 2. The believer himself? God the Father? 4. God the Son? 5. God the Holy Spirit?

We think we can do without Reverend "So-and-so" by accepting the concept that it is not water baptism that is referred to here.

We think we can do away with the believer himself as the baptizing agency. The verb is not reflexive; it is passive, and the passive is used to describe something that is done to us, not something we do to or for ourselves (i.e., Jesus was baptized by John).

We believe that we can eliminate God the Father. We know of no reference that would support the concept of the Father doing the baptizing. The Father is not named as the baptizer in any verse with which we are familiar.

God the Son as the baptizing agent is a possibility that is taken seriously by some people. We could go along with this to some extent if it were baptizing only into His death. It is conceivable that Christ might baptize us into His death, but the implication of the text is that we are baptized into Christ, and therefore we are baptized also into His death.

The concept of Christ baptizing into Himself is contrary to what we feel we know concerning the economy of the Godhead. The Father is glorified by the Son, the Son is glorified by the Spirit. There is an element of humility latent in that picture which the idea of Christ baptizing into Himself destroys.

The agency of baptism would certainly seem to be the Holy Spirit. This is strengthened by the idea of the body as it is set forth in 1 Corinthians 12:12ff. "For just as the body is one and has many members, and all the members of the body, though many, are one body, so it is with Christ. For by one Spirit we are all baptized into one body—Jews or Greeks, slaves or free—all were made to drink of one Spirit." This is an application of the figure of speech Paul has used in the tenth chapter concerning the "baptized" Israelites and their drinking from the same rock. "For by one Spirit we are all baptized into one body." He is saying that when the Holy Spirit baptizes us into the body of Christ, we no longer live in the singular. "Now you are the body of Christ and individually members of it" (1 Cor. 12:27).

The following two paragraphs are technical, and if you have been going along with us, you may wish to skip them, but for those of you who have an interest in the details of the 1 Corinthians 12 passage, we might add something further.

There are those who translate the verse not "by the Spirit" but "in the Spirit." We have no argument with this, provided the agency of the Spirit is not destroyed (i.e., by and in the Spirit). It is the same grammatical problem that appears in 1 Corinthians 6:2, "The world is to be judged *by* you" (authors' italics). This is the same preposition *(en)* followed once again by a passive verb. If you want "in the Spirit" in chapter 12, then make chapter 6 read, "The world is to be judged in you." We think that "by" is the simpler translation in both cases. When the New English Bible uses "in" in chapter 12, and "before you" in chapter 6, it does not necessarily destroy the concept of agency.

Here is an example. An Englishman may say, "I came to London by train." He means that he came to London in a train. However, if he had not had the money for the fare and had been forced to "hitch a ride" on the roof of the passenger car, he would still say, "I came to London by train." It is a preposition of agency.

One of the passages that seems to us to show the universality of the baptism of the Holy Spirit in terms of all believers is in chapter 10 of Acts. Here, while Peter was still speaking to the Gentiles, the Holy Spirit "fell on all." (Granted it does not say baptized, but in chapter 11 of Acts, Peter describes his experience to the Jerusalem church, and he equates the Gentile experience to the experience at Pentecost.) As far as the text is concerned, nothing is shown to precede the giving of the Spirit to the Gentiles. If nothing precedes it, how can it be a second work of Grace?

We would suggest that apart from the Holy Spirit's baptizing a person into Christ (in this present age), there is no forgiveness of sins. Apart from the Spirit's baptizing a person into Christ, that person cannot be a new creation. There is a reason. All the blessings stem from our union with Jesus, and this union can take place only through the baptizing work of God the Holy Spirit. He puts us into Christ. (The phrase "in Christ" or "into Christ" appears in

Life Because of the Spirit

the writings attributed to Paul approximately 164 times. To Paul it seems to have been important.)

We would like to say that rather than a second work of grace, the baptism of the Holy Spirit of the believer into Christ is the foundation upon which all else that follows is built. "For in Christ are all the riches of God's grace." Notice that it says "all."

May we be permitted to make our case a little stronger by an argument from silence. (That is not "ironclad logic," but sometimes it is inductively useful.) As we noted above, John the Baptizer spoke of Jesus who would come after him and baptize with the Holy Spirit and with fire. Just before Jesus ascended to be with the Father, He told His disciples that they would soon be baptized with the Holy Spirit. Never again, after that time on Mount Olivet, have we any record of the disciples or anyone else being told to look forward to the baptism of the Holy Spirit. There are other uses of the word "baptism," and there are other functions and experiences of the Holy Spirit, but nothing is said concerning the baptism of the Holy Spirit as being that which is to be sought. It is assumed that the believer received the baptism when he believed "into" Jesus Christ our Lord.

In Romans 6 Paul assumes his reader's spiritual baptism as the basis for the daily walk with Jesus expected of every believer. This baptism is the reason for the ending of the complete dominion of sin over his life. It is the basis of the outward demonstration of fellowship with Jesus, without which a man cannot claim with confidence that he belongs to Christ.

In chapter 12 of 1 Corinthians referred to above, Paul tells his readers that they were joined to or made part of the body of Christ as a result of the baptizing ability of the Spirit. If some members of the church had received the baptism of the Holy Spirit as a second work of grace and some members had not, how can his analogy be justified?

Please let us repeat. After Pentecost, the baptism of the Holy Spirit is nowhere presented as something which the believer into Christ is told to seek. It is presented as something which has happened to those who are "in Christ."

---

*If you want a scholarly comment on this point, look in the *International Critical Commentary*, Romans 6:5.

4. The Spirit in Us

Now let's look at some of the other verbs mentioned in connection with the Holy Spirit. In some passages of Scripture, men and women are said to be filled with the Spirit of God.

In Luke 1:41-42 it states that Mary, about to become the mother of Jesus, visited her cousin Elizabeth who was about to become the mother of John the Baptizer. Mary greeted her cousin and when Elizabeth heard Mary's salutation the fetus leaped within her womb; and Elizabeth was filled with the Holy Spirit and spoke out. After Elizabeth's baby was born and the baby's father, Zechariah, had obeyed the angel and named the baby John, the text says that Zechariah was filled with the Holy Spirit and prophesied.

The Unpredictable Wind

Notice that these experiences are pre-Pentecost. It seems to us that Jesus equates the baptism of the Holy Spirit with Pentecost. It does not seem advisable therefore to say that being filled with the Spirit and being baptized by the Spirit are necessarily the same thing.

However, the word "filled" is used post-Pentecost also (Acts 4:8), when "Peter, filled with the Holy Spirit, said to them . . . ." Again in verse 31 "When they had prayed, the place in which they were gathered together was shaken; and they were all filled with the Holy Spirit and spoke the word of God with boldness." In Acts 6 when there were complaints among the believers about the distribution of charity, the apostles said to pick seven men who were reputed to be honest and wise and full of the Holy Spirit and they would appoint them to handle the business.

May we be permitted to deduce from this that being filled with the Spirit seems to be a condition in which the will of the individual is completely surrendered and the Holy Spirit "takes over" to do or to say something in accordance with His will? Note one difference, however. In the case of Elizabeth and Zechariah the implication seems to be that the filling was temporary. It seems to have been for a short period of time; it was therefore punctiliar and for a particular act. Contrarily, the filling of the men in the

The Spirit in Us

sixth chapter of Acts looks as though the "filling" is (ideally) a characteristic of a continuing, growing influence, and therefore linear. These men were habitually surrendered. A point might be made to the effect that filling before Pentecost was punctiliar, while filling after Pentecost could, in some men at least, be a continuing thing. We will have more on this later.

One factor is true in all cases. An act was to be performed or work was to be done that could not be done in the "flesh." The Magnificat of Mary the mother of Jesus (Luke 1:46-55) is great Hebrew poetry and magnificent praise to the Almighty rivaled by only a few of the Psalms. To assume this is the product of a seventeen-year-old Hebrew peasant girl who is not recorded as having written anything else before or after is a little hard to believe—far harder, in fact, than to believe that the Spirit spoke through her.

The seven men chosen to serve table in Acts 6 faced more than is commonly realized. There were two kinds of Jews in the church in Jerusalem, and the tension between them was great. They closed ranks only in the face of Samaritans. To distribute money or food among Jewish women who for years had formed two groups that despised each other and to distribute it in such a way that peace and tranquillity followed is not a distribution done "in the flesh."

The Unpredictable Wind

Men who were beaten in accordance with the Law (as Peter and John were beaten for preaching Jesus), if they prayed at all between screams, prayed to God to bring an end to the agony. Instead, these men asked to be given the courage to earn another beating. Our opinion is that they were filled with the Spirit.

It looks to us like a two-way street. A man or woman may be given a task and be filled with the Spirit to perform or to endure. Or, we may submit to the Spirit as best we can in the depths of our souls and then being so qualified chosen for a task. Maybe we will be told to wait on tables. If we are filled and chosen for that task, waiting on tables will be a source of both temporal and everlasting blessing.

We should return now to the passage we discussed briefly in chapter 2, the passage concerning the Samaritans. Let us look at Acts 8:14ff." . . . when the apostles at Jerusalem heard that Samaria had received the word of God, they sent to them Peter and John, who came down and prayed for them that they might receive the Holy Spirit; for it had not yet fallen on any of them, but they had only been baptized in the name of the Lord Jesus."

Those who teach the "second blessing" route have an easy time with this. If you read it casually, it seems to fit their picture neatly. The Samaritans believed, were baptized, and became "Christians," but they

The Spirit in Us

had not received the Holy Spirit. The picture that is sometimes painted is that Peter and John came to Samaria, prayed, and laid their hands on the Samaritans. Then the Holy Spirit "baptized," and tongues, signs, and wonders appeared. This sounds good.

But there is one little difficulty with that picture. Some signs and wonders preceded the receiving of the Holy Spirit. Simon was amazed before the apostles came (Acts 8:13), "And seeing signs and great miracles performed, he was amazed." May we suggest that these signs may not have been the sole property of Philip. The words are not singular.

The complete picture, then, is that Philip's ministry produced conversion, water baptism, *and* signs and wonders, but no Holy Spirit.

(Let's be honest. This story does not fit our pretty picture too well either. This may be a good sign. We are a little suspicious of doctrines that fit all texts. If God had wanted a systematic theology, He would have had one written instead of the Bible. The Scripture has its paradoxes, and to deny this is pharisaical blindness.)

There is one interesting interpretation that helps some people. They point out that the primary meaning of the Greek word *lambano* is "take" and not "receive." Using the primary meaning of *lambano* the verse could be made to read "who came down and prayed that they (Samaritans) might take (rather than receive) the Holy Spirit." In other words, that Peter and John came down to pray that the Samaritans would do their bit and reach out and take what was theirs by right of regeneration. One trouble, we cannot find one Greek scholar, believer or unbeliever, who will translate it that way for us and we are a little unhappy with unique translations that help us teach our doctrine.

Let's stay as honest as we can. This passage does not quite fit the way we would like it to fit, but the above suggestion about *lambano* opens the door to another possibility with which we can be happier. There is a contribution to be made by the Samaritans.

Looking at 1 John 2:11 we read, "But one who hates his brother is in darkness. He is walking in the dark and he has no idea where he is going" (authors' paraphrase). Anyone who hates his brother has darkness, and it can happen, at least temporarily, to any of us at any stage of our spiritual lives. When we walk in the dark, the evidence of the nature of Jesus, the evidence of our spiritual baptism is blocked out, at least for that time.

Philip preached, and conversions were there, baptisms were there, signs and miracles where there, but the nature of Jesus did not shine through. Hate was there also. Jew and Samaritan were at each other's throats. There was something the Samaritans

The Spirit in Us

and the Jews had to do. The Jews had to swallow their terrible pride and self-righteousness and go to Samaria and actually put their hands on a Samaraitan (a dog to a Jew). They had to do it so that the hated Samaritan might receive the Jewish God.

The Samaritan had to eat his intense hatred of the Jew, accept men from Jerusalem (a city whose spiritual authority he refused to acknowledge, John 4:20) and receive a blessing from the hands of those whom he despised. He had to accept a Jew as his brother in the Lord Jesus Christ.

When this happened, they were dipped in God's "vat" and came out dyed the color of Jesus. The evidence of the Holy Spirit's baptism was then present. It is our guess that at this point Simon Magus saw, for the first time in his life, unmitigated joy.

We do not want to press this point; we just hope it helps, but whether this Samaritan explanation has any value or not, it does contain one factor that we are going to pursue a little further. There is an area of responsibility that belongs to the believer as far as the Holy Spirit is concerned. We are commanded to be filled with the Holy Spirit. Ephesians 5:18 is the first text that comes to mind. "Do not get drunk with wine, . . . but be filled with the Spirit."

It seems foolish to us to try to believe that a command was given that no one is capable of obeying. The believer has some part to play in the filling of the

Spirit in his life. Let's look at some of the possibilities and some of the signs of this "filling" in the next chapter.

5. Life in the Spirit

In chapter four we mentioned a possible difference between being filled with the Spirit in a punctiliar way (brief or limited time only), as compared with being filled in a continuing or linear sense. There are two words in the Greek text with slightly different meanings that tend to show this difference. Unfortunately both words are frequently translated with the one English word "filled." The translators of the New English Bible have tried to bring out the difference between the two words. For example in Ephesians 5:18 they translate the first Greek word so as to imply cooperation on the part of the believer, "but let the Holy Spirit fill you"; while in Acts 2:4 the second Greek word is simply translated "they were filled."

The Unpredictable Wind

As usual, there is one text that does not quite fit our picture. John the Baptizer is said to be filled with the Spirit from his mother's womb. That sounds pretty linear, but the punctiliar word is used. We are going to "cop out" on that this way. A man's life is a fixed period of time and therefore, in a sense, punctiliar. Also, in keeping with the other uses of the punctiliar word, he was given an assigned task to perform. (If that is not too sly, let it pass.)

In all fairness, the two concepts are in the New Testament: (1) a temporary filling for a particular task or a trial to be endured, and (2) a sense of continued filling that should be characteristic of the followers of Jesus.

We are commanded to be filled with the Spirit. How do we do it?

First, remember that the Holy Spirit does not come by law. The third chapter of Galatians states emphatically that the Spirit is supplied and miracles are worked among the Galatians because of hearing with faith and not by keeping the law. We do not strive and work ourselves into the place where God can trust us with some of His Spirit. The Holy Spirit is not given to the believer to reward him for his faithfulness or his maturity. He is given to the believer because without the Holy Spirit the believer would never know or experience faithfulness, love, or any semblance of maturity. But that still does not

Life in the Spirit

answer the question. How does one get filled and, hopefully, stay filled?

Acts 4:23-31 may contain a helpful suggestion. Peter and John were arrested for preaching Jesus. They returned to the other believers after their release and told what had happened. The believers prayed, and the place was shaken. They were all filled with the Holy Spirit and spoke God's word boldly.

It says they prayed, but it does not say that they prayed for the Holy Spirit, nor did they pray to be filled with the Spirit. They prayed that the servants of Jesus be given the power to do something, to speak out for Jesus boldly—not boldly in the flesh (God forbid) but boldly in the power of the Spirit.

They were not thinking of their own merits nor were they calling them to God's attention; they were thinking of God's love and mercy and of the necessity of spreading the news concerning it. As far as we can tell from the text, they were not even asking for this power for themselves, but for Peter and John. It was an unselfish prayer by those who were preoccupied with God's working, God's power, and God's glory. The result was that *all* of them were filled with the Holy Spirit, and *all* of them spoke the word of God with boldness.

If you have accepted the sacrifice of Christ for your sins and experienced repentance, if you have surrendered your life to Jesus, and if you want to do His will, we believe you have been baptized by the Holy Spirit into Christ. No natural man can do these things. Now lay hold of the Spirit by faith; He's in you.

Granted, there is a catch, and maybe this illustration will help us explain it. Stacey Woods says that the Holy Spirit is the world's most unique "hitchhiker." He stands beside the road of your life, asking to be let in, but when you stop to pick Him up, He will not get in unless you let Him drive. There's the rub.

We cannot get the Holy Spirit by good works, but we can shut Him off by being disobedient. We can have an experience with the Holy Spirit (more about that later), we can become filled with His presence and love, and the glow can slowly or quickly die. We are not "filled" any longer. Things go back to "normal."

Let's go back to the hitchhiking example. We stop our life, we let the Holy Spirit in, and He does the driving. At this point we are excited about Jesus, His work, and His glory. Then we notice something. The direction in which the Holy Spirit is driving is out of "Egypt." We remember something "Egyptian" that we would like to have on our trip. We reach for the wheel and turn our life around. We are not all wrapped up in God's glory at that particular moment, and joy begins to fade. Something else fades, too —humility.

One of the surest signs of the presence of the Spirit is humility, not modesty, which is based on self-consciousness, but humility which is characterized by unselfconsciousness. One of the surest signs of our "quenching" the Spirit is the return of our pride. We begin to think again that in our own strength we can "do something for God." Confidence in our abilities returns. The Holy Spirit climbs into the back seat and patiently waits until we know we are lost. When we realize we are lost, we say so, and we give Him back the wheel. Once more we are occupied with His way. Joy and some humility return, and "Egypt" is again behind us. We are bound for the promised land.

We are told to be filled with the Spirit. But the New Testament does not teach that we are to be filled only once so we can have a happy and exciting experience to look back on, nor should we consider yesterday's filling sufficient for today. We should surrender as much of ourselves as we can see to surrender and do it as constantly as we can. This is so that we will not interfere with God's pouring His Spirit into us by being disobedient. We receive His blessing when His Spirit is directing us and choosing our paths.

What we have touched on here is really a separate subject, namely, the question of knowing what is

The Unpredictable Wind

God's will for us. Before we continue with our main theme, we would like to pause and say something about God's guidance. Books on "how to know the will of God for you" are frequently a mixed blessing. It is difficult if not impossible to "codify" the relationship between the individual and the Holy Spirit. It is like trying to set down rules for a successful marriage. Successful marriages do have things in common, but they have great differences also. In the same way "successful" Christian lives have things in common, but paradoxically one of the things they have in common is their uniqueness.

We are told in Romans 8:14 that the sons of God are those who are led along by the Spirit. How do we know the leading of the Spirit? We do not believe there is a definitive answer to the question. Any attempt to give one is apt to be a return to the principle of law, a principle that Paul condemns so completely in Galatians. All we can do to try to be helpful is to say that there are ways in which the Holy Spirit works in our lives.

One of His most common tools is the giving of an inner peace after guidance has been sought by conversational prayer with the Father or with Jesus. Also, He can and does speak to us through Scripture, through others who are following Jesus, through the fellowship of believers, through circumstances, and through principles of God's nature which are revealed in Jesus Christ. He can, when He wants to do so, work through the godless as well. (See 2 Kings 24:2.) He will use these, or any combination of them, including all or none.

It might be helpful to put it negatively. If we have reached the place where we want the will of God (the leading of the Holy Spirit), if we have prayed for it and sought it, regardless of the cost, if in this framework we cannot find it, then there is no hope for any of us. But we can find it. He promised to reveal His will to His servants, and He keeps His promises. Do not fall into the trap of thinking you can stipulate His methods. Sometimes we do stipulate, and He graciously lets us "get away with it," but it is poor practice. He is God, He is sovereign, and He can deal with us as, how, and when He sees fit.

There are signs of His dealing. Signs that come when we are in the center of His will, signs that we can see particularly when we look back on our life in Him. One sign is the giving and filling of the Spirit. He longs to do this, for He wants to reach out through us. The Spirit is not just "given." He is said to "flow through" the believer. In the words of Jesus (John 7:38ff.) anyone who believes in Him, out of that believer will "flow" (constantly) rivers of living water. He tells us here that He has reference to the Holy Spirit.

Our filling should be the same as that which

characterized the men of Acts 6, a filling which was continuous and observable to the other believers. By our preoccupation with the Lord and His works this can be done, but it is not easy. A wilderness journey never is. The Red Sea is deep, and the desert is hot and dry.

He knows this, and He gives gifts as well as His presence to help us on our way and to help us let Him do the driving. These gifts are for blessing and for service and we would like to talk about them as gently as possible.

If you have your heels dug in and your jaw set against the giving of any particular gift, you might just as well put the book down and forget it. We appreciate your position on the basis of personal experience. But our own attitude has had to be altered. We are among those who found their theological fortifications undermined and we have had to change a little. We hope to stay in the position where we realize that someday we might have to change a little again. We are learning, and we would like to share with you the little we know. It is not a shallow subject, and maybe we will still be looking into the nature and work of the Holy Spirit if and when we reach the Presence. We will go right on learning. After all, John the Beloved got his surprises (Rev. 1:17).

We have a friend who is the minister of a Fundamentalist church. He believed that the gifts of the Holy Spirit were for the first-generation church only and were apostolic in nature. He put together a sermon on this matter. He testified later that it was the best sermon, most filled with Scripture, best thought out that he had ever put together. He preached it with great pride.

The trouble was that during his quiet hour the next week he prayed in an unknown tongue. The following Sunday he got up and told what had happened to him. He apologized for the preceding Sunday's sermon. Need we point out that this was disquieting to all concerned? Some people withdrew their membership.

His life has not been greatly changed. He knew Jesus and was following Him before and after his experience. He had already been baptized by the Holy Spirit into the body of Jesus; it is just that the God of all comfort gave him a gift to help him through a very trying experience that God knew was on its way.

It is time here for us to insert a word of warning. Remember we talked about the three-legged stool; the water and word, the blood, and the Spirit. Any one of them can be misused. The Old Testament prophet Isaiah warns against the misuse of Scripture. "The word of the Lord will be to them precept upon precept . . . line upon line . . . here a little, there

The Unpredictable Wind

a little; that they may go, and fall backward, and be broken, and snared . . ." (28:13ff.). This means that the written word itself, if used by us to justify our sins, can itself become a trap.

Jesus warns against the misuse of Scripture (John 5:39). "You search the Scriptures because you think that in them you have eternal life. But they testify to me and you do not come to me" (authors' paraphrase).

Like the written word, the blood of Jesus can be a danger (if we are on our "own trip" somewhere doing our "own thing"). There are those who count on the blood of Jesus to cleanse them from sin even though they walk apart from Him and in darkness. This does not seem to be what the text says to us (1 John 1:9).

Unfortunately, we have to say something similar about the Holy Spirit. He, too, can be made into a one-legged stool. The gifts and calling of God are not revocable, i.e., He does not necessarily have to take them back (Rom. 11:29). God gives and He blesses. We may do with the heavenly vision whatever we will. This has led to some very tragic situations.

One man, gifted in teaching to an extreme degree, a man who wrote what may be the greatest life of Christ outside of Scripture, died, as far as anyone can tell, a raving blasphemous atheist. But to his dying day, we believe that he could still teach. We think this because one of the authors of this book received

Life in the Spirit

great spiritual benefit from his scholarship and his teaching.

The Spirit of God and the gifts of the Spirit of God can form the most dangerous of the one-legged stools. Few believers would argue that because a man could quote hundreds of Bible verses, he was thereby assured of a saving fellowship with God. Few believers would argue that a man or woman living cheerfully in flagrant and open adultery can lightly claim that the blood of Jesus is washing away all sin. (There are some Christian theologians who do so argue, but they are a small minority indeed.) Yet there are those who feel that because they exercise a gift of the Spirit, real or imagined, they are thereby proven to be properly related to Christ. As the Gershwin song goes, "It ain't necessarily so."

It is interesting to us to note that the Book of 1 Corinthians, which deals with the matter of supernatural gifts, particularly "tongues" (we are going to discuss this gift in detail further on), also deals with flagrant sexual sin (1 Cor. 5:1ff.). It is dangerously true that the use of a supernatural gift of the Holy Spirit can let a believer lead himself into a point of cockiness where he thinks he can get away with almost everything. He is far from the Spirit of God, but the gift sails on and on.

Paul warns against this. He says that if a man has the gift of tongues, so that he can speak in the unknown tongues of men and of angels, it can be sounding brass signifying nothing if love is gone (1 Cor. 13:1).

Agreed, we have been taking something for granted here, and that is that the gifts mentioned in the New Testament are available to the Christian today. Not everyone agrees with this, so we will look at the problem in the next chapter.

6. Gifts from the Spirit

In chapter 12 of 1 Corinthians there is a list of gifts credited to the Holy Spirit and distributed by Him throughout the church. Among the gifts are wisdom, knowledge, healing, administrations, and so forth. One of the gifts listed, "tongues" or something called "ecstatic utterance," has been a center of controversy within Christendom for centuries, starting with the trouble in the church in Corinth. The misuse of this gift is one of the reasons Paul wrote what we call 1 Corinthians.

It is human nature to throw the baby out with the bath water. An entire theological school came into existence based on the assumption that all the gifts, anyway all the blatantly supernatural ones, were a first-century experience only, that after God arranged the writing and distribution of the New Testament, the need for such gifts diminished and gradually passed out of the life of the church. Those who follow this school of thought want no part of the gift of "tongues" or anything else that is like it.

There is a widely held point of view that is completely opposite. Believers, loosely grouped under what is called "the Pentecostal Movement," have their minor differences, but basically they hold that all the gifts listed in the New Testament are to be used today. Arguments about these gifts have ripped churches, destroyed marriages, and fostered more hate than anything since the Spanish Inquisition. The tragedy is that there have been wonderful believers in both camps who have been crushed and embittered by the conflict. It is so unnecessary. The authors of this book have fellowship in Christ with people who hold these opposite points of view —granted, not with the fanatics in either camp, but with those who follow Jesus, holding for the moment one view or the other. Our fellowship should be based on the life we have in common, the life of Jesus, and not on the question of whether or not the Holy Spirit worked differently in one century than He did in another.

Most of the arguments about the gifts have hinged on the argument about "tongues," so let's talk about

Gifts from the Spirit

it for a moment. Basically it means that a man is speaking in a language he does not understand. In the New Testament there are at least three forms mentioned. On the day of Pentecost, the disciples spoke in tongues they had never learned, but the listeners understood what was being said.

In 1 Corinthians 12, there is a difference. No one understands the tongue being spoken unless someone in the congregation is supernaturally gifted to interpret. The speaker himself does not understand.

We do not want to get into a big discussion of religious anthropology, but there seems to be need for a few words along that line here. Man is divided, at least functionally, into three categories in the New Testament: body, soul, and spirit. The following statement is a gross oversimplification, but it will help for the moment. With the body, man makes contact with what he calls "the real world." With the spirit, he has a capacity to experience God. With the soul, he has a mediating factor that includes, among other things, the power of decision and of reason.

In 1 Corinthians 14:14 Paul says that when he prays in an unknown tongue, his spirit prays and his tongue prays, but, as the King James quaintly puts it, "My understanding is unfruitful"; that is, the soul, or the soul function of reason is set aside, and the body of the individual is used to pray and so is his spirit.

The Unpredictable Wind

This seems to us to make possible a third kind of "tongues" gift. If man's reason is set aside, could he not pray or speak in an angelic "tongue" (1 Cor. 13:1)? Such a practice might be well beyond the range of human reason, but not necessarily beyond the range of human spiritual experience.

Because of these scriptural references, there is little argument among believers concerning tongues in the early church. They were used. The present-day argument about the gift is twofold. One, are tongues used today; and two, if they are, what is their significance?

There is a passage in 1 Corinthians 13 that says these tongues of ecstasy will cease. The trouble is that the same passage implies that knowledge will pass away at the same time. Those most anxious to rid the church of tongues are usually least anxious to rid it of knowedge, particularly theirs. The case against tongues today is a weak case. The gift is listed alongside the other gifts of the Spirit, many of which are in evidence in many places. We can see no biblical argument for separating this gift, or other similar gifts, and giving them an early burial. We can see plenty of argument against their misuse, and we will come back to that later.

The second question, "What is the significance of tongues?" is a more hotly debated matter. Some of the Pentecostal groups, but not all, have claimed that

Gifts from the Spirit

the only acceptable evidence to a believer that he has been baptized by the Holy Spirit is his initial (and possibly only) ecstatic utterance. It is at this point that the fur begins to fly.

As we read the Book of Acts, we can see where the Pentecostal position gets its strength. It certainly looks as though tongues and the baptism of the Spirit go together. However, there is one mitigating factor that is not always pointed out. Tongues, the gift of so speaking, was a prophesied promise to the Jew. It was to enable him to believe that the Messianic prophecy had been fulfilled. It is to this prophecy that Peter makes reference in his Pentecost sermon.

Paul also refers to the Jewish heritage. Speaking of the purposes of tongues, he says (1 Cor. 14:21ff.), "In the law it is written, 'By men of strange tongues and by the lips of foreigners will I speak to this people (i.e., Israel) and even then they will not listen to me, says the Lord.' Thus, tongues are a sign not for believers but for unbelievers."

Let's try to paraphrase what we think is his argument. Paul is saying that God promised Israel signs to authenticate the Coming One. One of the signs was the gift of speaking in strange tongues. The Messiah came. One evidence for this is the occurrence at Pentecost, when men stood and simultaneously fulfilled the prophecy, speaking all at once and in several different languages.

The Unpredictable Wind

Although hundreds of men were baptized into Christ on this day and the body of Christ began to take form, the failure that is prophesied also took place. The nation of the Jews as a whole officially refused to acknowledge Jesus as the Messiah. Therefore, although Paul is careful to make provision for restricted use of tongues in the fellowship, he says at this point, "It is a sign for the unbeliever (Jew). Now don't imitate Pentecost in your church service. It's the wrong place, the wrong way, and for the wrong people" (authors' paraphrase).

In Acts, where there were Jews to be convinced concerning the giving of the Spirit and the authenticating of Jesus, tongues are mentioned. On the day of Pentecost, almost all those present were Jews. In the house of Cornelius there were Jews who could not bring themselves to believe that the Spirit could be given to Gentiles, not until they heard tongues. The disciples of John the Baptizer were, by tradition, Jews, and they were given tongues at the time they received the Spirit. It is interesting that in Samaria, where there were no Jews to convince (Peter, John, and Philip were already convinced), there is no mention of tongues. Another argument from silence, perhaps, but in keeping with the quotation from Paul in 1 Corinthians 14.

We used the verb "baptize" in its connection with the Holy Spirit to mean the joining of men into the

Gifts from the Spirit

body of Christ, and changing their nature to begin to conform to Jesus. We would like to use the term "filling" to describe further experiences with the Holy Spirit. For signs concerning filling we need not look to tongues and tongues alone:
- Acts 4:8 and 4:31, the sign of a filling is speaking the word with all boldness.
- Acts 7:55, Stephen's filling is demonstrated by his ability to pray for his murderers.
- Acts 13:9, Paul, filled with the Spirit, condemns a false teacher.

Stronger than all these is the passage in 1 Corinthians 12:18-31. It states emphatically that the gift of tongues is only one of many gifts manifesting the Spirit's presence. Paul wrote this passage because believers in Corinth were making the difference between gifts given to each believer a source of division amaong themselves. Certain gifts were looked up to more than others, and believers with more spectacular gifts were more highly regarded within the fellowship. This was an anathema to Paul. "Many gifts, many members, that's fine, *but* only one body and only one Spirit." He insists that they reverse their thinking, "On the contrary, the parts of the body which seem to be weaker are indispensable" (12:22).

This may be why Paul says that the church must not forbid "tongues" (1 Cor. 14:39). In the list of gifts in 1 Corinthians 12:28 it seems to be the weakest gift, but if it is the only one a believer has, he must not be put in a context where he is not permitted to use it. Where its use (even the greatly restricted use Paul stipulated) is forbidden, is it not possible that some other things the Holy Spirit brings with Himself are also excluded, such as joy?

Notice, we said forbidden. This is different from voluntary restraint. There are men and women with this gift who will not use it in a public meeting because of unpleasant connotations connected with its misuse. (More on this later.) "All things are lawful, but not all things are expedient."

They say, " Why use something good when it will be thought to be evil and cause strife?" Their position may be well taken, and we would not argue with it, for it is clear that this gift, like the others, is under the restraint and discipline of the believer so gifted, and the Holy Spirit (1 Cor. 14:32). The gift is not to be forbidden; it can be restrained.

Tongues are obviously not a universal gift nor a universal experience. In 1 Corinthians 12:30 Paul asks if all speak in tongues. The implication is clear that the answer is no. He does not say, "except of course for your initial experience with the Spirit." In 1 Corinthians 14:5 he states that he wishes they all spoke in tongues. If the gift or experience were universal, the sentence would be pointless. Even stronger, concerning the importance of the gift, is the last half of the same sentence, "But even more to prophesy."

Paul also gives one evidence of the Spirit even more important than prophesying, "I will show you a still more excellent way" (1 Cor. 12:31). Love is placed first, and prophecy second (1 Cor. 14:1-2). Prophecy (literally, speaking for God in an intelligible language) and love build up the body of Christ. Tongues may build up the individual believer (1 Cor. 14:4), but it is abundantly clear that their misuse tears down the church. This is what has fueled the antagonism to the gift, but before we look at the negative side, we would like to present one more affirmative consideration.

We do not want to be personal or embarrass anyone so gifted, so we are going to make a composite. This is an imaginary person who combines real characteristics of real people whom we know and have heard "pray in a tongue."

Our composite is thoroughly educated, a doctorate from a first-rate secular university, a professional man, a man who has followed Jesus for years. He has never used his gift in a public meeting. When asked about the use and purpose of tongues, he had something like this to say:

"Sometimes I come home from the office, tired, discouraged, and in no mood for prayer or fellowship with the Lord. I go into my bedroom and kneel down and pray in a tongue. When my spirit is refreshed and I feel peace return, I switch to English and talk to the Lord with my mind, too."

Who would want to deny such an experience? Who would want to deny it to anyone to whom it had been given? No wonder Paul could wish all the Corinthians spoke in tongues.

Now for the negative side. Down through the years in our experiences with Pentecostal people and Pentecostal groups we have noticed that the problems connected with the misuse of the gift seem to follow the pattern evident in the book of 1 Corinthians. 1. Tongues were being misused, chapters 12-14. 2. Sexual immortality was present and openly acknowledged (1 Cor. 5:1ff.). 3. Women had a public and authoritative ministry in the church (1 Cor. 14:34-36). All three are condemned.

In the few cases that we have experienced where there has been an *unhealthy* emphasis on tongues, the other two factors have been present also.

May we soften point number 3 just a little. It seems that when Paul talks about women keeping silence in church, it has to do with teaching or explaining. Provision is made in chapter 11 for a woman to prophesy or pray in church. The requirement is that she have her head covered. Let us explain that further.

Gifts from the Spirit

In many parts of the world, even today, and particularly in Spanish-oriented cultures, if a woman enters a bar or other public place, sits down, and takes off her hat, she is probably a prostitute, and taking off her hat is a way of soliciting business. Apparently this was true in the Corinthian culture also. When a woman was married or had a liaison with a particular man, she wore some type of head covering (called a veil in the King James), which was sometimes fastened to the hair on her forehead with a clasp. When she was "playing the field" she went around with her head uncovered.

It would seem that the women in the church in Corinth, when they began to follow Jesus, decided that the sign of servitude to a man was beneath their newfound dignity. Therefore, when they came to church they removed their "veil" or head covering. Paul is aghast for two reasons. First, any man visiting the meeting for the first time would certainly get a false impression of what was going on, and Paul says, "For heaven's sake, put your hats back on."

The second objection is that Paul teaches that the woman in Christ is subject to the man in Christ. Now before you throw the book down, remember that there is a distinction in Scripture between function and ontology, or being. The President of the United States, theoretically, is the same before the law as the rest of us, but as far as the country is

The Unpredictable Wind

concerned, do we all have an equally important job?

In Christ there is neither Jew nor Gentile, slave nor free, man nor woman. This is ontological. But some men have more important responsibility within the fellowship than other men; this is functional. Men are given authority over women, but the authority is functional only. When a man thinks he is more important because his function is more important, he is holding a thought that borders on the Satanic. So is the woman who, conversely, thinks her function is just as important as if she were a man.

Paul does not permit a woman to teach or hold authority, and she can pray or prophesy only if she is publicly admitting a subservient functional relationship to a man within the fellowship.

This does not sit well with our culture. It did not sit well with the Corinthian culture either. There was a "women's lib" movement at Corinth that had attained equality with men in secular and many religious circles and apparently there were women who wanted to bring their secular equality into the church and function as men.* Paul will have none of it and insists on an order that he says is established by God. This order is always out of phase with every culture. Satan will twist it one way or the other; he does not care which way. If he makes the woman functionally equal to the man, he has upset God's order. If, in some other culture, he makes chattel of women, he has upset God's order in the opposite direction. Do not expect sympathy and understanding from the godless concerning Paul's teaching about woman in the church. The natural or unregenerate man does not receive nor understand the things of the Spirit of God.

One more negative aspect of the gift of tongues should be mentioned before we leave the subject. There are imitations. In a secular university there was a professor of psychology whose father had been pastor of a Pentecostal church. The professor hated the gospel in general and tongues in particular.

He brought a patient out of a local mental institution to a class in advanced psychology. This man, before his illness, had been prominent in the tongues movement. The professor placed the sick man in a chair facing the class. The patient was partially catatonic and did not turn his head. The professor wrote the clichés of the Pentecostal world on the blackboard behind the patient, i.e., Holy Ghost, Baptized with Fire, Tongues from Above, and so forth. The class could see the words. Then the professor picked up the morning newspaper and began to read a secular article from the sports page, only at the end of each sentence he added a word from the blackboard. It went something like this:

"Joe Blow, fullback for the Cardinals, carried the ball over the ten-yard line, Holy Ghost. It gave the necessary impetus to the team to score, Baptized with Fire. The opposition never recovered sufficiently to offer a serious threat for the rest of the game, Tongues from Above."

In a few minutes the patient began to show signs of agitation and broke out in ecstatic utterance at the top of his voice. It was the professor's way of showing that "tongues" is a form of self-hypnosis that can be triggered. He was right. It sometimes is and it sometimes can be. But this is what the logician calls the error of the undistributed predicate. "All cows are four legged (almost all cows, anyway), but not everything with four legs is a cow." Some ecstatic utterances are the product of self-hypnosis, but this does not prove that all ecstatic utterance is the product of self-hypnosis.

Let us admit that there is a psychological factor in "tongues." There must be—there is one in every human activity whether it is divinely inspired or not. But that does not mean the psychological factor is all there is.

C. S. Lewis has a beautiful illustration that explains this. Let's say that two men are listening to a pianist play a piano arrangement of a Wagnerian opera. One of the listeners has never heard an opera, nor ever heard anything but a piano. The other listener is a conductor who has memorized the opera. If the conductor turns to the uneducated listener and says, "That part's for the French horn, that part's for the tenor, that part's for the violins," the man who has never heard an orchestra is going to call for the strait jacket. The uneducated listener can prove scientifically that there is nothing playing but a piano.

There is a psychological factor in all of God's dealings with us: conversion, regeneration, tongues, and all else. The man who is not born again cannot see the kingdom of God, and the psychological factor is all he will see, and he can prove it scientifically. That does not prove that there is nothing else there. The unbeliever has no previous experience or knowledge to bring to his observations. All he can hear is the piano. If you have had any experience with the Spirit of God, you know about violins.

---

*William Baird, *The Corinthian Church—A Biblical Approach to Urban Culture*, (Nashville, Abingdon Press, 1964) p. 121ff.

7. The Spirit in the Fellowship

In the preceding chapter we changed from talking about the relationship of the Holy Spirit to the individual believer, to the working of the Holy Spirit within the born-again-collective. That "born-again-collective" is a fancy term, but we do not like to use the word "church" for reasons that will become obvious as we go.

The passage in Hebrews 10:25, "Not forsaking the assembling of ourselves together, as the manner of some" (KJV) has been used like a club by many ministers trying to increase attendance at their Sunday morning church service. The writer of Hebrews may have had a couple of completely different things in mind, and we will get to them in a page or two, but

The Unpredictable Wind

first a word about the conventional eleven o'clock service and its appendages.

If you are a follower of Jesus, do not "knock" the Sunday morning "bit." God has used it, and He can use it. Sometimes it is a necessary way to avoid commitment. Remember our quoting Paul when he spoke in the synagogue, "Men of Israel, and you that fear God." The "God fearers" were on the edge. They did not want to become Jews, but they wanted to hear about God, and the situation was greatly used when Paul came along. Many of these God fearers become pillars in the first fellowships. Some people have to hide from God (and other people) while they find out about Him, and the "church" can be a good, impersonal place in which to do this.

If you put an uncommitted man in a small group fellowship of dedicated and consecrated believers, you may force him to choose between following and not following Jesus before the Holy Spirit has prepared him to make that choice. Granted, God can and does use the impact of a consecrated group also (1 Cor. 14:25), but He does not always do so.

Think of the "church" or an "evangelistic service" in terms of the parable of Jesus in Luke 8. A sower went out to sow seed. Some fell on the path, some on stony ground, and so forth. In His explanation of His parable, Jesus prophesies that much of the "word" that is sown is not going to bring forth fruit, but

The Spirit in the Fellowship

some of it will fall on "good ground." Many a man or woman has taken a first tentative step toward the kingdom of God through a hymn or a sermon that has within it that which fills the momentary need. If the "church" were not being used, it would not be here.

We are not mixing "use" with blessing or approval, God does not bless everything He uses, nor does He approve of everything He uses. In Matthew 7:21ff. we read, "Not every one who says to me, 'Lord, Lord,' shall enter the kingdom of heaven . . . . On that day many will say to me, 'Lord, Lord, did we not prophesy in your name, and cast out demons . . . and do mighty works in your name?' And then will I declare to them, 'I never knew you; depart from me, you evil-doers.' " If you have a ministry, real or imagined, and that passage does not scare you just a little, you have a problem.

We are not trying to suggest by the above that everyone in the "church" is weak and ignorant of the things of God. God wants a witness to Jesus in every part of the world, even the religious world, and there are those who stay within the framework of the Catholic or Protestant church out of obedience to the Holy Spirit. It is not up to us to try to judge what is going on in the life of many a servant of Jesus. (Rom. 14:4, "Who are you to pass judgment on the servant of another?")

The Unpredictable Wind

To those of us who have difficulty with any kind of fellowship within the organized "church," the words of Jesus to Peter may apply. "Never mind them; you follow Me." Following Jesus is "the name of the game."

As we mentioned above, when the writer of Hebrews talks about not neglecting fellowship, he may have had two things in mind. They are both helpful in the Life in Jesus, but before we discuss them notice that we did not include fellowship in our "three-legged stool." There are three legs; the water and word, the blood, and the Spirit. We did not make it four legs and include fellowship, because fellowship is a blessing and a privilege that is denied many who follow Christ.

How can a man or woman who is in prison, in solitary confinement for years, be expected to obey a command to fellowship? Such a person has a three-legged stool (including Scripture that the Holy Spirit may bring to mind), but that is all there is. It may be, though, that such prisoners have one common and essential characteristic. Those who have survived such treatment and lived to record it, all claim to have missed terribly the fellowship of other believers. Hebrews tells us to remember those who are imprisoned, as though we were in prison, too. It is a dreadful experience. Fellowship with other believers is a wonderful part of the life that is ours in Christ.

The Spirit in the Fellowship

The New English Bible does not always use the word "fellowship" where the Revised Standard Version does. They have changed it, and we think the change is for the better. "If we walk in the light we share a 'common life.' " This is a little different than "If we walk in the light we have 'fellowship.' " People can have fellowship at a Rotary Club or an alumni association or on a street somewhere. It can be good fellowship in terms of conviviality. This is not necessarily the same thing that is being discussed in 1 John.

We talked about the fellowship or common life of the Father and the Son in the first chapter of this book. It is in some way related to their common life with God the Holy Spirit. With the believer something similar happens (Matt. 18:20), "Where two or three are gathered in my name [more accurately, in my interests] there am I in the midst of them." This is the work of the Holy Spirit in the corporate life of the body of Jesus. He makes Jesus real among us in a way He does not make Jesus real to us individually. When two followers of Jesus find their paths crossed and sit down in a cafe for a cup of coffee and begin to talk about how Jesus is working in their lives, they build each other in Christ. God the Holy Spirit is ministering to them as they minister to each other.

This is one kind of "assembling together." There is another kind the writer of Hebrews may have had in mind. It could be that which is described in 1 Cor. 14:26, "When you come together, each one has a hymn, a lesson, a revelation, a tongue, or an interpretation. Let all things be done for edification."

Admittedly, there are other kinds of "meetings," if you want to call them that. For instance, Paul argued in the synagogue. He rented the Hall of Tyrannus and argued the things of Jesus daily. He preached at the Areopagus. He even preached to an assembly of believers. In chapter 20 of Acts, we read that Paul ". . . prolonged his speech until midnight." (May we suggest that if you feel qualified to preach long sermons, that you, like Paul, had better have the ability to raise again to life those who fall asleep and kill themselves.)

However, the exercise of the public gift and its use are balanced by the experience of the common life in Jesus. This common life is usually shared in the type of meeting described above by the apostle Paul. These meetings and the gifts brought to them have a life-giving purpose. Let's start with the concept of the "hymn." It can objectively demonstrate what we are trying to expound. When a group of believers assemble and sing about Jesus (and they did this from the first), they bring into existence a sound that none of them can individually produce. One voice is too nasal, another has too little nasality; one voice is

The Spirit in the Fellowship

over-resonant, another has none at all; one tends to sharp, another tends to flat; but together they make a beautiful thing. Take fifty or sixty young people who love Jesus and who have sung together for months (preferably, but not necessarily, without instrumental accompaniment), and listen to them, and you will see that the whole is equal to more than the sum of its parts. The Holy Spirit is there, too, and He is ministering in a way that He does not normally minister to any one of us singly. He is building the body of Jesus. This is the purpose of all the "gifts" of the Holy Spirit.

He is dealing with us individually to increase the image of Christ within us. This image is the fruit of the Spirit, love, joy, peace, and so forth. Then He gives us a "gift" with which the corporate body of Christ is built. This is the purpose of the gift.

Let's point out two characteristics of these gifts. First, as mentioned above, the gift is to build up the body of Christ. Those of us who use our gift, teaching, tongues, or any other, to bring glory or attention to ourselves may find ourselves someday before the judgment seat of Christ, holding a crown made of dust and ashes. First Corinthians 14 is very clear, "Don't show off."

The second characteristic of the gifts is that they begin where human resources cease. There is a difference between natural abilities, abilities with which we were born or abilities we have developed on the one hand, and gifts of the Spirit on the other. God can and does use both. Notice that He makes this distinction in Matthew 25:14ff., "For it will be as when a man going on a journey called his servants and entrusted to them his property; to one he gave five talents, to another two, to another one, to each according to his ability." The talents are the property of the wealthy man and are handed to the servant as something distinct and different from natural abilities, but the natural abilities are also taken into consideration. God uses both the natural and the supernatural.

It was the same in the earthly ministry of Jesus. Natural ability was certainly there, but so was spiritual power to the ultimate degree. This spiritual power was used where natural gifts leave off. He was gifted to heal, but there is no record of His going around using this power to remove splinters or to cure hangnails. There is, however, the example of the woman who had been sick for years and spent all her worldy goods on physicians. She was still sick, and Jesus healed her. His power was brought to one who was helpless and, apart from Him, completely hopeless.

It is the same today. Both the authors of this book have been involved in situations in which the Holy Spirit, as a result of prayer, healed. But in every instance medical help was not available, or the case was beyond the scope of medical knowledge. We do not believe that God puts the gift of healing into a fellowship to make it unnecessary to take an aspirin. The primary use of the gift of healing within a fellowship is to preserve the life or health of a member so that that member may continue to use his or her gift to build the body of our Lord Jesus Christ and to glorify God.

What is true of healing is true of the other gifts also. A man may have the human ability to teach. He may study and prepare himself to do so. He may teach, but the body of Christ is not formed, or if the assembly is there it is not built up. He has ability, yes, but the gift?

Paul says that the God of this world has blinded the minds of those who do not believe (2 Cor. 4:4). Lieth Samuel once said, using his beautiful British accent, that a supernatural hand has pulled down the blind (shade), and only a supernatural hand will be able to raise it. The "ability" to teach applies equally to all subjects. The gift of teaching applies to raising the blind through the presentation of the word so that Jesus is seen. This is a "talent," and it comes from the Holy Spirit.

What does it mean to "build up the body of Jesus"? What is supposed to be accomplished? May we make a suggestion?

The Unpredictable Wind

In Revelation 2:17 we read, ". . . and I will give him a white stone, with a new name written on the stone which no one knows except him who receives it." It is helpful but not necessary to think of this stone as a mirror. It reflects something unique. We would like to suggest that the thing that is unique is a facet or a characteristic of Jesus which can be seen with complete clarity only by that individual. It may be that the "bride" of Christ will be complete when God has shaped believers, one by one, to reflect clearly all the facets of the nature of Christ. When all facets are reflected, the real church is complete.

God shapes us many ways, starting biologically. Paul speaks of God separating a person from his mother's womb, implying the design and plan of God from the beginning. He shapes us also by our contact with the world in which we live, but He counteracts the undesirable elements of this influence two ways: first, by the Holy Spirit reshaping us individually and bearing "fruit"; and secondly, He shapes us in our contact with each other in our corporate sense.

The ultimate assembly or "church" is described in Hebrews. It says that Jesus is not ashamed to call us brothers but sits in the midst of the congregation leading praise to the Father.

As we see it, Christ in His glory is surrounded by the multitude that is perfectly recreated to reflect that

The Spirit in the Fellowship

glory, and all glory is then raised to the Father. Ideally the local, temporal "church" or assembly is reflecting in an imperfect manner the scene that is yet to come. This is the reason we must all contribute in some way to the meeting. In us, some measure of Christ is being built for a fitting into the final assembly. This may be why there is no provision in Scripture for *a* pastor or *a* teacher. Rather the New Testament says pastors and teachers. (No mention of assistant pastors either.)

There is one *the* pastor, and there is one *the* teacher, the Messiah. The plurality of teaching without one final human authority in the group permits the Holy Spirit to teach as He sees fit. We like to think that as we teach the Scriptures that God has hung a filter in front of our mouths, which directs one sentence to one individual and another sentence to another. The human teacher presents information. The Supernatural Teacher takes it, filters it, and conforms it more to the image of Jesus.

A larger number of individuals contributing means that more facets of Jesus can be exhibited, for what is true in the ultimate assembly is partly true in an earthly assembly. Some of us can see some things about Jesus because of the uniqueness of our being. It needs to be shared, and the real Jesus, still seen through a glass darkly, is made a little more clear to all. The body is thereby built up.

It means that we are under an obligation to contribute. It also means that we are under an obligation to keep silence upon occasion, for the spirit of the prophet is subject to the prophet. This means discipline, self-discipline and the discipline of the Holy Spirit, for "all things are to be done decently and in order." God is not the God of confusion.

This is God's way, and with few exceptions we are to join ourselves to one another, two, three, ten, or a thousand and share a common life—the Life of Jesus. This is done by our Advocate, Comforter, Counselor, revealer of Jesus, God the Holy Spirit.

8. The Spirit and the Law

We are going to conclude with a chapter on the relationship between Law and the Holy Spirit. This is the oldest conflict in Christianity. It caused the first church "split" (Acts 15:1ff.): "But some men came down from Judea and were teaching the brethren, 'Unless you are circumcised according to the custom of Moses, you cannot be saved.' And when Paul and Barnabas had no small dissension and debate with them, Paul and Barnabas and some of the others were appointed to go up to Jerusalem to the apostles and the elders about this question."

Circumcision is not the only problem. If you are a "Spirit-filled follower of Jesus," what is your relationship to the Old Testament? What is your relationship to the Mosaic Covenant? More specifically, what is your relationship to the Ten Commandments? Are you bound by them? If the answer is no, are you free to commit murder? If the answer is yes, why don't you "Remember the seventh day to keep it holy"? The keeping of the seventh day is one of the Ten Commandments, too. (The reasoning by which the seventh day of Moses becomes the Sunday of the Christian is reasoning that no sane logician can follow. "Six days shalt thou labor, and on the seventh. . . .") The last day of our week belongs to the Lord, according to the law, not the first. When we look into Paul's opinion on the matter, things are further confused. He says we may treat all days the same if we wish (Rom. 14:5).

If this kind of problem has never troubled you, set the book aside. We do not recommend taking aspirin unless you are feeling pain. If you do not care about a problem, the answer is of little interest. Furthermore, we don't propose to put to rest forever a question which has troubled the followers of Christ for about two thousand years. This is a complex matter, and this chapter will not be easy reading. If you do read it, when you are through think about what we have presented in the light of what the Spirit is presently showing you. If you cannot see what we're talking about, forget it. For if you learn from us apart from the Holy Spirit, you'll be wrong even if we happen to be right.

The Spirit and the Law

To start with, Paul has some nasty things to say about those who teach "Law" as part of faith in Christ. Much of it is in the Book of Galatians. "For freedom Christ has set us free. . . . I testify again to every man who receives circumcision that he is bound to keep the whole law. You are severed from Christ . . ." (5:1ff.). He even goes so far as to suggest that those who preach the Mosaic Covenant as part of the gospel of Christ, and therefore also advocate circumcision, should go further than circumcision and cut off their sex organs (5:12). This is strong language. Even a cursory reading of the Book of Galatians will show that Paul had no time for the mixture of the Holy Spirit and the Law (3:2). His message is clear, that Christ is the end of the Law.

In what seems at first glance to be a flat contradiction to this are the words of Jesus in Matthew 5:17ff., "Think not that I have come to abolish the law and the prophets . . . but to fulfill them. . . . Whoever then relaxes one of the least of these commandments . . . shall be called least in the kingdom of heaven. . . ." This statement seems to put Paul at the very bottom of the heap.

There are those who try to resolve the conflict by making a distinction between "ceremonial law" and "moral law." They claim that when Paul says we are free from the Law, he means the ceremonial part of it, and that the moral law, i.e., the Ten Commandments, are still binding.

There are a couple of problems with this position. When Paul is discussing the Law from which Christ sets him free, he picks one of the Ten Commandments, "You shall not covet" (Rom. 7:7). So, the example given of "law" from which we are freed is "moral" and not "ceremonial." This makes the supposed distinction not quite credible.

Also, Jesus does not seem to recognize any such distinction. In Matthew 12, when Jesus is accused of violating the Sabbath, one of the Ten Commandments, His defense is an appeal to the action of King David in eating "the bread of the Presence." Now if there is a distinction between the Ten Commandments and "ceremonial law," how can the violation of the bread by David (ceremonial) justify the violation of the Sabbath by Jesus (moral)? It doesn't fit.

One more problem. When Paul seems to contradict in 1 Corinthians 14:34 that which he preached in Galatians, we have an added complexity, "The women should keep silence in the churches . . . . They . . . should be subordinate, even as the law says." Is this "moral" or "ceremonial"? Either way, how do you reconcile it with Galatians 3?

It would seem to us that there is a possible explanation in the ambiguity of the concept of "law." Law is used in at least two separate and distinct ways in our own culture. A posted speed limit of 55 miles per hour is one kind of law. The law of gravity is

The Spirit and the Law

another. The speed limit is an ordinance and can frequently (but not always) be violated with impunity (i.e., "You drive, and I'll watch for the fuzz").

But, a man who has jumped from a window on the fiftieth story of a building does not seem to have the same option. He may have several seconds during which he may regret his act, but the consequences of it are rarely avoided. One consequence is never avoided. He will get to the next object below him within his trajectory. This is an observed regularity, and in that sense and that sense alone it is "law" to the unregenerate man. In the opinion of the godless, no one passed the law of gravity. It's just here.

For the sake of convenience, let's call "law" in the sense of observed regularity (i.e., the sun is usually seen first in the east) natural law. Let's call "law" in the sense of regulation, (i.e., don't spit on the sidewalk) ordinance, clearly two meanings for the same word, "law."

Right here we can solve one issue. Parallel ordinances are not binding. There is such a thing as separate jurisdictions. Let's illustrate. It is not fair for the legalist, the person living under Law, to say to the man free from the Law, "Can you commit murder?" The man free from the Law has to reply, "Of course not." Then the legalist can triumphantly say, "See, you are still under the Ten Commandments." No dice.

The Unpredictable Wind

If the legalist asks, "Are you free to commit murder?" the proper answer is no, it is against the laws of the Dominion of Canada.

To this the legalist replies, "What's Canada got to do with it? We don't live there."

The reply to that is, "We're not Jews, and we don't live in Israel either." The fact that Life in the Holy Spirit does not permit murder does not mean that it is because of the Hebrew Law, no matter how universally that law may be applied throughout the world. The man in Christ lives in another kingdom. More on this later.

This still does not rid us of our internal New Testament conflict, the conflict between law, laws and the Holy Spirit.

Let's pursue our divisions of "law" a little further. From the point of view of the theist (there is a God) these observed regularities or natural laws are really "laws" in both senses. We believe that God established them. This leaves us with no problems as far as miracles are concerned. So the axe head floated? So Peter walked on the water? That's easy, the One who wrote the law rewrote it.

That sounds great, but it is too simplistic. It tears down the significance of the temptation of Christ. He was asked to turn rocks into bread to serve His own purposes and needs. He refused for several reasons, one of which is that He was acting as repre-

The Spirit and the Law

sentative man and was self-restricted by laws that govern a human being perfectly related to the Father.

Why, then, did He walk on water? C. S. Lewis has an intriguing answer. Lewis says that on rare occasions and when no one was present who was not already committed to the truth, Jesus allowed the "laws" of the next world to shine through for a moment into this one.

Whether you "buy" that or not, in the public ministry of Jesus and as natural man, He stayed within the framework of life as it is ordained. Fish came from fish, bread from bread, and wine from water.

The Psalmist says, "The heavens are telling the glory of God; and the firmament proclaims his handiwork" (19:1). We think he is saying that God's physical world shows some measure of His personality as He wants us to see it.

We believe that beside physical laws which show His personality, there are underlying moral laws that show His character. It is here that the conflict between Law and the Spirit begins to dissolve.

Let us look at an example and then work back from it. In Matthew 19 the Pharisees are testing Jesus on the matter of divorce. When Jesus says no to divorce, they quote Moses and Moses' bill of divorcement. Jesus answers in a very interesting way. "Because of the hardness of your heart, Moses permitted you to divorce your wife, but from the beginning it was not so . . . God made them one man and one woman" (authors' paraphrase). In effect, Jesus is saying that the Law of Moses is "relaxing" God's moral law.

Now when we turn back to Matthew 5:17 it has an entirely different meaning. "Whoever, then, relaxes one of the least of these commandments. . . ." What commandments? The underlying moral order of the universe that reveals the nature of God. It is revealed to us in what Jesus is teaching in the Sermon on the Mount. The way to relax the commandments of Jesus ("these commandments") is to go back to the Mosaic Law. We will give further evidence later, but for the moment let it stand.

If we do let it stand, the contradiction in Paul disappears. When Paul talks about the subservient position of woman as given in the law (1 Cor. 14:34), he may not be referring to the Mosaic Code and to the legal righteousness which he condemns in Galatians. Paul may be referring instead to that which precedes Moses, to the way in which the moral nature of God is revealed through moral law that begins with the story of Adam and Eve. "From the beginning it was not so. . . ." The use of such precedence leads us to another point about basic, pre-Moses and post-Moses moral law. It is that which undergirds the universe and it, too, is immutable, just like gravity.

Let's go back to our illustration of the man jumping out of the fiftieth-story window. If he wants to, he can yell all the way down, "There is no gravity, there is no gravity." He will not have to shut up until the ground silences him. So, too, the immoral and self-indulgent man, prosperous and pleased with himself may say, "There is no moral law, there is no moral law," all the way to the grave. Scripture says that the wages of sin are death. You may protest this to your dying day, but no longer. Moral law, like the law of gravity, ultimately takes its toll. It is fulfilled when we die.

Let's back up a little and come at this problem from another angle. Jesus said He would fulfill the Law. There is a first and obvious way. In our business offices we have files full of contracts. We pay no attention to them. They are fulfilled. We agreed to buy, accept delivery, and pay. We did so. Both parties are satisfied, the contract is fulfilled and set aside.

Christ fulfilled the contract of the Law. When He said, "It is finished," it was finished. But there were two things which were finished. The Mosaic Covenant with its demands and its ordinances (Col. 2:14) was all through. But the thing that underlies the Mosaic Code was also fulfilled. Jesus brought it to the level where it needed to be brought to show forth the moral nature of God. He did this with His teaching, with His life, and with His death.

The Unpredictable Wind

Now for "the further evidences" we promised. These evidences will take the form of comparisons. The ordinance demands that a man tithe (give a tenth of all he earns). Jesus told the rich young ruler to give away all that he had. Also He taught that if a man takes our coat we are to give our cloak also, and we are never to turn away a beggar. The ordinance says to remember the seventh day, to keep it holy. Jesus teaches that every moment of every day belongs to His Father (John 5:17). The Old Testament gives permission to hate one's enemies; Jesus demands that they be loved (Matt. 5:43-44). The ordinance says an eye for an eye, a tooth for a tooth; but Jesus said that if you are hit on one cheek, turn the other for the same treatment. And so, "ad nauseum." This leads to the following question.

Which is easier, to keep the ordinances or to do as Jesus taught? Which relaxes which? To most of us it would seem that the commands of Jesus are far harder than anything in the Old Testament. This is why Jesus can finish His remarks on the subject by saying that unless our righteousness exceeds the righteousness of the Pharisees and the Doctors of (Mosaic) Law, we shall never see the kingdom of heaven. Their lives were based on Mosaic Law and their traditions. These "water down" or "relax" the real law of God.

How then can Paul, without putting his tongue in

The Spirit and the Law

his cheek, rejoice at his deliverance from the Mosaic Covenant? It seems like being happy over leaving the frying pan for the fire. The Ten Commandments are something we cannot keep—who among us has never coveted anything? How are we going to fare when we are judged by the standards of Jesus as proclaimed in His Sermon on the Mount?

It is here that the ministry of the Holy Spirit enters in terms of Law. Let's go back to the rich young ruler (Luke 18:18). When Jesus told him to sell all he had, give it to the poor, and follow Jesus, the man turned away sorrowing for he had much wealth. At this point Jesus noted that it was harder for a rich man to get into heaven than for a camel to go through the eye of a needle. (Pastors of wealthy churches and professors of heavily endowed seminaries have been rewriting that passage for years. Don't let them throw you. Read it like it is, or the rest of the conversation doesn't make very much sense.)

Peter is aghast. "Who, Lord, can be saved?"

This is a shrewd question, and it showed that Peter got the point. If you condemn the rich, you will have to condemn those who wish they were rich. God looks on the heart. Peter was a man who could exhibit a little greed. One day, when he got really greedy, he nearly sank his boat (Luke 5:7). If the rich young ruler was eliminated for being rich, Peter knew that in all justice he, Peter, had to be eliminated for trying his best to get himself to the "top of the heap."

The Lord's answer is profound. "That which is not possible to man is possible to God." This is an early reference for regeneration, to Pentecost, and to the baptizing and filling by the Holy Spirit. The Lord's demand in Luke 18 is impossible to a normal, self-centered human being, but the demand is fulfilled in Acts 4:32. "Those who believed were of one heart and soul, and no one said that any of the things which he possessed was his own. . . . There was not a needy person among them."

The point that Jesus is making in the story of the rich young ruler is that nothing can fulfill the moral demands of the divine nature except the divine nature. After Pentecost the Holy Spirit brought into the believer some small portion of the divine nature as He baptized the believer into the body of Christ.

"That which is not possible to man is possible to God." It is not human to be unconcerned about wealth. It is true that great philanthropists have given away huge sums of money, but they were conscious, as far as we can tell, of the fact that they were giving. This is why they allow themselves to be called great philanthropists. There are even those who for the sake of their fellowman have impoverished themselves, but were they not conscious of what they were doing? Did they not consider it virtuous?

The Spirit and the Law

It is little difference if a man is rich, or proud of being poor, his preoccupation is still money. Unself-consciousness is a quality of the man who has become truly conscious of God. He can reach this point in some measure when God is not only without, but within.

All the other demands of Jesus, all that go beyond the ordinances to the true Law, are fulfilled in only one way. Only the divine nature is divine. Only the man filled with the Spirit can keep these "laws," and he can do so only to the extent that he is filled with the Spirit.

Let's look at a paradox which to us is inexplicable on any other basis than the one which we have stated. In Matthew 15, Jesus is accused of violating the traditions of the elders. He would not wash His hands before eating, after being in the marketplace. (We doubt that He was objecting to cleanliness. It seems that the Jews were in the habit of washing, lest they had touched a Gentile or some other unclean thing. To have washed would have given credence to their standard.) His answer to their accusation was a counter-accusation. "The law of God says, 'Honor your father and mother,' but you say that a man may give to God what his parents would otherwise get, making void the law of God."

It is not as anti-religious as it sounds. There may have been a trick to it. The man could use for himself

The Unpredictable Wind

alone that which was "given to God," material things that should have been shared with his parents, until the man himself died. Then what was left, if anything, went to the temple. It was a very selfish arrangement. The word for pulling this stunt was call "Corban."

In the seventh chapter of Mark the same argument is recorded, only this time Jesus says, "For Moses told you to honor your father and your mother," rather than "God said to honor your father and your mother." This seems to equate the Law of God and the Law of Moses. However, things don't get really complicated until we get to Luke 14:26 where Jesus says, "No man can be my disciple unless he hates his father and his mother" (authors' paraphrase). There is not any softer word for "hate" either. Hate is what He said.

The equating of the "Law of Moses" with the "Law of God" is no big problem. We need only remember what was said above about "parallel ordinances not being binding" (our Canada-Israel illustration). As there are similarities between life under Mosaic Law and life in the Spirit, similarities which do not necessarily make Moses binding on life in the Spirit, so there are similarities between Moses and the revelation of the will of God that preceded "the Law." Certainly the greatest example of "honoring your father" in the Old Testament is Isaac's acquiescence to the

The Spirit and the Law

sacrifice of himself at the hand of his aged father. This incident precedes Moses by hundreds of years. However, the third passage (Luke 14:26) ordering us to hate our father and mother, and so forth, is not as easily explained.

In passing, C. S. Lewis says that the command to hate father and mother was addressed not to those who find it easy, but to those who find it impossible. If it is easy it may be a biblical excuse to do what we want to do and would be a terrible sin. It becomes the modern day "Corban" of the Pharisee.

Jesus' command to hate father and mother falls in the context of 1 John 2:7, "Beloved, I am writing you no new commandment, but an old commandment which you had from the beginning" (to love one another). The command to love comes first and last (1 John 2:8). "Yet I am writing you a new commandment . . . because the darkness is passing away and the true light is already shining." The oldest light in the world is God for He *is* light, but He is hidden by sin, law, religion, man's nature. Now the oldest light is the newest for it is shining again through the Spirit in the revelation of the Life of Jesus as shared in the Spirit.

May we give an actual illustration? We have a young friend, a Methodist minister, who, together with his lovely wife, decided that God wanted them to drop out of the church and start an orphanage.

They already had three children of their own. By the end of the first year, they had added about a dozen orphans, and there were fifteen children in the house. Friends of ours, who had never before met them, visited the orphanage for an entire day. At the end of that time, our friends got the ex-minister off into a corner to question him. The conversation went something like this:

Friend: "O.K. I give up."

Ex-minister: "Give up on what?"

Friend: "Which three of these fifteen kids are yours? You treat them all the same."

Ex-minister: "That's because all fifteen of them are." With a grin, he pointed out the three that were his biologically and therefore had a double relationship.

The biologically based love for his own three children (which is basically selfish) had been swallowed up in the "Love of God" for all the children. It is our opinion that the command "to hate" does not apply to him nor to his wife, for in them the tug of biological relationships that come between us and the will of God had been absorbed into the first commandment (Thou shalt love). They loved with the "Love of God."

When Jesus said (Matt. 10:36), "A man's foes will be those of his own household," He meant the biological household, not the household of God. This

The Spirit and the Law

is the only explanation we know for the words of Jesus in Luke 18:29. They come at the close of His discourse concerning the rich young ruler, "there is no one who has left house or wife or brothers or parents who will not receive back more than a hundred times in this life, and in the age to come, eternal life" (authors' paraphrase).

How can God give you one hundred parents in this life? The same way He gave our ex-minister friend fifteen children. He had three biologically, but fifteen (at least) by the Spirit. We are back to the first chapter of 1 John, "We share a common life." When God puts His nature into us through the filling of the Spirit *all* brothers are our brothers, *all* parents are our parents. The Law to "honor" is pointless, and the command to hate the "natural" is unnecessary (Rom. 8:2ff.): "The law of the Spirit of life in Jesus Christ has set you free from the law of sin and death." The law will find its fulfillment in us whose conduct is under the control of the Spirit.

Love is the fulfilling of the Law, but the Spirit is the source of love. The man who is filled with the Spirit is free from law in the sense of ordinance. Not that the Old Testament is irrelevant. It is filled with illustrative material about God and how He works (1 Cor. 10:6). But it is no longer binding. It is fulfilled in the sense of ordinance by the death of Jesus. The real message at which it hints is fulfilled in the Life of

Jesus. The real message is also reflected in some small measure by those whom God has filled with the Holy Spirit. The person who is filled and submitted to the Spirit is reflecting the true nature of God which underlies the universe. By the Holy Spirit he is in touch with reality.

This still leaves us with one question: Is fulfilling the law, even the Law of Love, really freedom? Is it not still law? Is not the command to "be filled with the Spirit" still a command? Is it not still law? Where's the freedom?

Let us ask a couple of questions along this line. If a man is starving to death and you put food in front of him, are you not able to say, "Feel 'free' to eat?" If you put a cup of cold water in front of a very thirsty man, is it so wrong to say, "Feel 'free' to drink all you want"?

If we are created to be God-centered but are self-centered; if we are created to be unselfish but are selfish; if we are filled with "uncreated" envy, spite, and lust, if these things are true and Christ gives us a hunger to be what we were originally created to be, can He not say concerning Himself and the Spirit that was sent, "The Son shall make you free indeed."

Free from what? Free from ordinances. Free from ourselves. Free from the dominion of sin.

"Free from the law, oh blessed condition" has its dangers. It can make the life in Christ look like one big joy-strewn path to glory. That life could be "joy-strewn" but it is not; it is narrow and hard. That is our fault. We keep going back to "Egypt" for something we think we want.

But there are moments in our lives when we are filled with joy and love, when we understand in part what God is doing for us and to us. These times are precious indeed for they, too, are a gift from the Spirit. They are times when we really love—not with selfish human love, but with the love with which God loves us. At such times, the Spirit can flow through us even as Jesus promised. He flows through like a cool stream in a blazing desert. At that moment, we are free to drink. At that moment we are free, for at that moment we love.

God made a receptacle called a human being. He had in mind something to put in it, His Holy Spirit. When He does this, we begin to become what we unknowingly, desperately desire to be. We are truly free of ourselves for His Spirit makes us truly conscious of Jesus.

"[The Spirit] has shone in our hearts to give the light of the knowledge of the glory of God in the face of Christ. But . . . [we have] this treasure in earthen vessels, to show that the transcendent power belongs to God and not to us" (2 Cor. 4:6).

Be filled with the Spirit.